Nope-Nope EMU

Written by R.C.Chizhov

Illustrated by Anastasia Yezhela

To Mom and Dad, who taught me to never give up — R.C.

Published by Blissful Conch LLC, Bradenton, FL.

10 9 8 7 6 5 4 3 2 1

Library of Congress Number: 2022907400

Publisher's Cataloging-in-Publication Data

Names: Chizhov, R.C., author. | Yezhela, Anastasia, illustrator.

Title: Nope-Nope Emu / written by R.C. Chizhov ; illustrated by Anastasia Yezhela.

Description: Bradenton, FL : Blissful Conch LLC, 2022. | 32 pages of color illustrations. | Series: Emu Town stories ; 1. | Audience: Ages 4-8. | Summary: When Emu loses the crown of fastest flapper in town, she starts saying "Nope!" to everything. A rhyming story about persistence and self-confidence.

Identifiers: LCCN 2022907400 | ISBN 9781737952633 (pbk.) | ISBN 9781737952640 (hardback)

Subjects: LCSH: Confidence -- Juvenile fiction. | Emotions -- Juvenile fiction. | Perseverance (Ethics) -- Juvenile fiction. | Picture books. | Stories in rhyme. | BISAC: JUVENILE FICTION / Animals / Birds. | JUVENILE FICTION / Humorous Stories. / | JUVENILE FICTION / Social Themes / Emotions & Feelings.

Classification: LCC PZ8.3 C45 2022 | [E]--dc22

LC record available at https://lccn.loc.gov/2022907400

Blissful Conch Publishing

"Let's play a game of emu-tag!"
"Nope, nope! I'll be the one to lag".

"Then how about a swim today?"
"Nope, nope! The waves are here to stay."

But she was once an optimist.
Back then, this emu did persist.
For strong-winged Emu loved to play
a game of emu-flap, they say.

And every year, she won the crown
for fastest flapper in the town.
Two hundred times, without a frown,
her wings would flutter up and down.

Then came a time of great surprise—
another emu won the prize!
Her wings had flapped, but much too slow.
She lost her game. Oh what a blow!

So from that day, all games were done.
No trying, doing, no more fun.
Afraid to fail, afraid to lose,
the safest bet was to refuse!

Until one day as Emu strolled,
she saw a monkey looking bold.
Reaching, stretching, grasping—why?
Monkey on a climbing try!

He dragged against the sturdy trunk,
but then he tumbled with a clunk.
In many ways, he tried to win,
and kept at it, not giving in.

Emu said, "You've tried enough, don't you see? It's very tough!"

"But I was born to climb a tree,
as it's my only home, you see.
I know I'll make it to the top,
and then you'll see my monkey-hop!"

Another day, as Emu strolled,
she saw a puppy looking bold.
Twisting, turning, spinning—why?
Puppy on a wagging try!

His tail was stiff and much too tight.
It did not wiggle, left or right.
In many ways, he tried to win,
and kept at it, not giving in.

Emu said, "You've tried enough, don't you see? It's very tough!"

"But I was born to wag my tail,
so there's no way that I will bail.
Now, I will surely find a way,
and then you'll see my doggy-sway!"

Another day, as Emu strolled,
she saw a spider looking bold.
Weaving, silking, threading—why?
Spider on a webbing try!

She crept and crawled but had no mesh,
and every time, she started fresh.
In many ways, she tried to win,
and kept at it, not giving in.

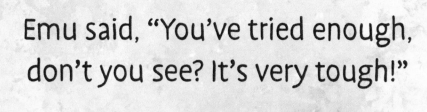

Emu said, "You've tried enough, don't you see? It's very tough!"

"But I was born to weave and thread,
to lay a trap for bugs to dread.
I'll spread the widest-ever net,
and then you'll see my spider-threat!"

Then Emu wondered, deep in thought—
what Monkey, Puppy, Spider taught.
Now, should she play her game once more?
And try to reach the highest score?

When emu-flap had come along,
the bird was ready, standing strong.
Waving, swaying, beating—why?
Emu on a flapping try!

At first, she flapped, but not as fast.
It seemed like she was coming last.
In many ways, she tried to win,
and kept at it, not giving in.

With all her strength and all her might,
she flapped on strong to win, all right!
Three hundred times, without a frown,
her wings beat swiftly, up and down!

The crown was hers! The emu won!
And now she wanted play and fun.

The emu who-can-munch-fast game?
"yes, yes! It may just bring me fame!"

The emu who-can-leap-far test?
"yes, yes! I'll try my very best!"

The emu three-toed stomping race?
"yes, yes! I know I have the pace!"

And **"yes I can,"** she said all day,
to any fun that came her way!

Made in the USA
Columbia, SC
20 October 2022

69497173R00018